Bjorn: To Lindsay, with love.
Many thanks to the Norwegian Illustration Fund for their valued support.

The Wolf's Whistle was initially conceived to be the first book in a series entitled: 'Behind the Tails' © 2010 Nobrow Ltd.
Written as a collaborative effort between Alex Spiro, Scott Donaldson, and Bjorn Rune Lie

Published by: Nobrow Ltd. 62 Great Eastern Street, London, EC2A 3QR
Typographic design by Natasha Demetriou

Order from www.nobrow.net
Printed in Belgium on FSC assured paper
ISBN: 978-1-907704-03-1

THE WOLF'S WHISTLE

BJORN RUNE LIE & CO.

O nce upon a time there was a wolf-cub named Albert. He lived with his dad, a salty sea-dog, in a small, crumbling house down by the docks. They were poor, they could barely rub two pennies together, but still every Saturday Albert's dad gave him a shiny coin to take with him to his favourite comic book store.

Albert loved comics, especially the ones about superheroes. He loved the adventure: the suspense, the secret identities and the special powers. But if comics had taught him anything it was the difference between right and wrong; good and evil. If someone was in need, Albert would always lend a helping hand.

As well as being a kind-hearted soul, Albert was also a gifted artist. Such were his talents that he had earned a scholarship at the very prestigious "Snobton Academy". Unfortunately Snobton was overrun by toffee nosed tigers and pampered poodles, arrogant elephants and spoilt hamsters.

Albert felt out of place, to say the least, but as luck would have it he was in good company. He had three close comrades who were all misfits of one kind or another: Chauncey, Libby and Vincente; mouse, stork and weasel respectively. They called themselves the "Fearless Four".

They were the firmest of friends, and whilst their fellow classmates would fawn over the latest and most expensive of toys, the Fearless Four would relish whatever they could chase, catch, find or make.

Every abandoned railway, forbidden rapid and disused warehouse was their playground. And the best part was: it was all free!

Although Albert loved such after-school tomfoolery, he was always preoccupied... his dream to become a star artist for Wonder Comics, the best comic book publisher in the universe, consumed his every thought. And each week, Albert would show his friends the latest pages from his own epic, "The Wolf's Whistle".

It was the gripping tale of a caped superhero called the Lone Wolf. This masked marvel would battle with bullies, defend the defenceless and could topple tall buildings with a single blow from his mighty lips. And in his most desperate hour of need he would call on his fearless sidekicks to help him battle his arch nemesis: the evil Dr. Chorizo.

Sadly the perils of these caped avengers were far from fictional. The friends had to battle real villains on a daily basis; three beastly bully brothers named Wade, Rafe, and Theron Honeyroast. They ruled the schoolyard with an iron trotter, and picking on Albert and his gang was by far their favourite past time.

One fateful afternoon, the Honeyroasts discovered the shoebox containing Albert's homemade Lone Wolf outfit. Snorting like crazy they tied the cape round his neck and shoved him out onto the playground. Everybody pointed and laughed so hard that Albert, tears streaming down his face, ran all the way home.

When his father heard what had happened, the old sailor scooped him up and said:

"Now son! I know it feels like your ship is sinking, and those boys have thrown the plug overboard... But always remember, you have a dream and that's your life raft!"

"I've never met a sailor worth his salt who gave a seagull's squawk about what anyone else thought!"

"Just follow your heart my boy. Map your course and set sail!"

The years went by, and Albert did indeed realise his dream of working for Wonder Comics. He was doing all sorts of jobs; making coffee, sorting mail, cleaning floors and scraping chewing gum from under desks. Everything but putting pen to paper! As he shuffled home from work on his 30th birthday, the thought of his empty refrigerator in his cupboard sized apartment filled him with dread...

But to his sheer delight he found his old gang there waiting for him, with cake, strawberry jelly and enough soda pop to sink a ship. "Happy Birthday, old cub!" they cried when Albert opened his front door.

It was a magnificent feast and afterwards the friends sat rubbing their gorged bellies with delight, reminiscing about their distant school days. When Albert asked what had happened to the hideous Honeyroast brothers, Chauncey squeaked: "Don't you know? Everybody in the city knows what they're up to, but I guess you've always had your head buried in your comics."

"They work for their dad, 'Al Prosciutto', the mobster. You must have heard of him! They're rolling in it, they own half the buildings in the city, including the one we live in. Nothing ever works; that's the reason it's so dreadful: they won't fix a thing."

It was true, the once great building that was the Old Printmakers, where his friends lived had fallen to ruin. There was a rumour that the Honeyroast brothers wanted to tear it down and develop the land, but that they couldn't because it was considered a local architectural masterpiece.

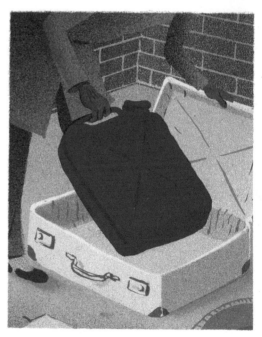

But it was crawling with cockroaches and the wall paint was toxic. It was like an icebox in the winter and a furnace in the summer, the roof was like a sieve and the fire escape had rusted to oblivion many years before. Chauncey, Libby and Vincente were the only tenants left in the building after a spate of freak accidents had driven everyone else away.

The Honeyroast brothers on the other hand, were living it up in the Ham-tons where they spent their days eating from golden troughs and their nights wrapped in silken sheets. Surrounded by hired goons, Wade, Rafe and Theron liked nothing better than to lounge around their pork chop-shaped pool drinking apple cider and stuffing their faces with white truffles.

Death Blaze not suspicious, says Chief Tenderloin

Freddy Tenderloin, the chief of police, told "the Daily Drivel" late last night that they are not treating the tragic fire as suspicious. The cause has been identified as a faulty toaster, which absolves the owners, Honeyroast Estates, of any blame.

Several properties belonging to the company have suffered a similar fate in recent years, but chief Tenderloin stresses this is purely coincidental given their large portfolio. He dismisses speculations about possible insurance fraud as "groundless and absurd". In a statement the company expresses its deepest sympathies for the families of the victims. A plan to restore the Old Printmakers, a grade 2 listed building to its former glory had been under way, but sadly the damage to the property is now too substantial from the wrecking ball.

Those gammony gangsters couldn't care less about anyone but themselves and god forgive anyone who stood in their way!

The morning after his surprise party, Albert had a spring in his step and he whistled a happy sea shanty as he walked into work. "How lucky I am to have such great friends", he thought, passing the newsstand. "No matter how bleak things might look I know I can always rely on…" Albert's heart stopped when he saw the headlines….

DAILY DRIVEL

HELLISH BLAZE KILLS THREE!

Three animals perished in a fire which swept through the historic "Old Printmakers" building on Porkobelly Avenue last night.

The victims have been identified as Chauncey Mouse, Vincente Weasel and Libby Stork, all tenants in the building. Emergency services were called around 11.30 Thursday, but the house was consumed by flames by the time they got to the scene. A faulty appliance has been identified as a probable cause. Arson is not suspected, the deputy Assistant Commissioner George Tenderloin

Albert rushed as fast he could to the smoking ruin. It was a terrible sight.

For all his years Albert had never felt so sad and alone. "Where are the superheroes when you really need them?" he sobbed. Just then a ragged old hobo came and sat down next to him. He put his hand inside his coat and pulled out a brown paper bag with a bottle inside it... "Here, have a swig of this", he said "It's mighty powerful stuff. It will give you all the strength you'll ever need... "

"Thanks", said Albert, but the hobo was already gone.

That night Albert slept a troubled sleep full of strange dreams.

At first it was muddled, but soon everything became clear.

Albert knew what he had to do. Without looking, he reached under his bed and retrieved a dusty old shoebox that hadn't seen the light of day for many years... Finally someone would be there to defend the defenceless, to topple the towers of tyranny and to huff and puff and blow all asunder who stood in the way of righteousness. Yes, Albert would become the Lone Wolf. Hear his whistle.